Mermaid Primary Composition Notebook

DRAW AND WRITE

+

COLORING PAGES

+

MAZES

this book belongs to

....

....

A B C D E F G H

I J K L M N O P Q

R S T U V W X Y Z

a b c d e f g h

i j k l m n o p q

r s t u v w x y z

1 1 1 1 1

1

1

2 2 2 2 2

2

2

3 3 3 3 3

3

3

4 4 4 4 4

4

4

5 5 5 5 5

5

5

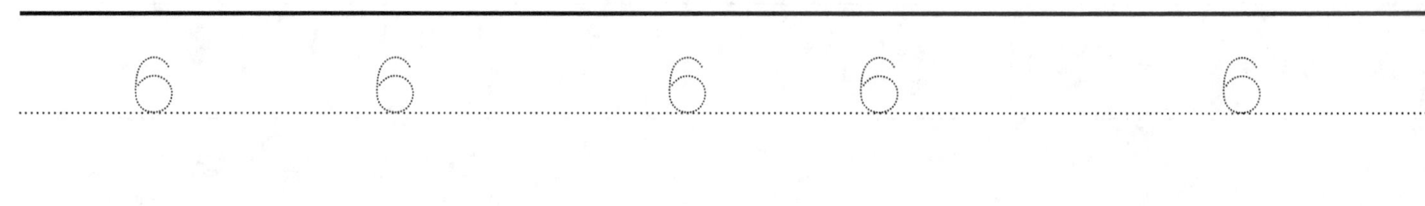

6

6

7 7 7 7 7

7 . . . .

7 . . . .

8 8 8 8 8

8

8

9 9 9 9 9

9 . . . .

9 . . . .

10 10 10 10 10

10 . . . .

10 . . . .

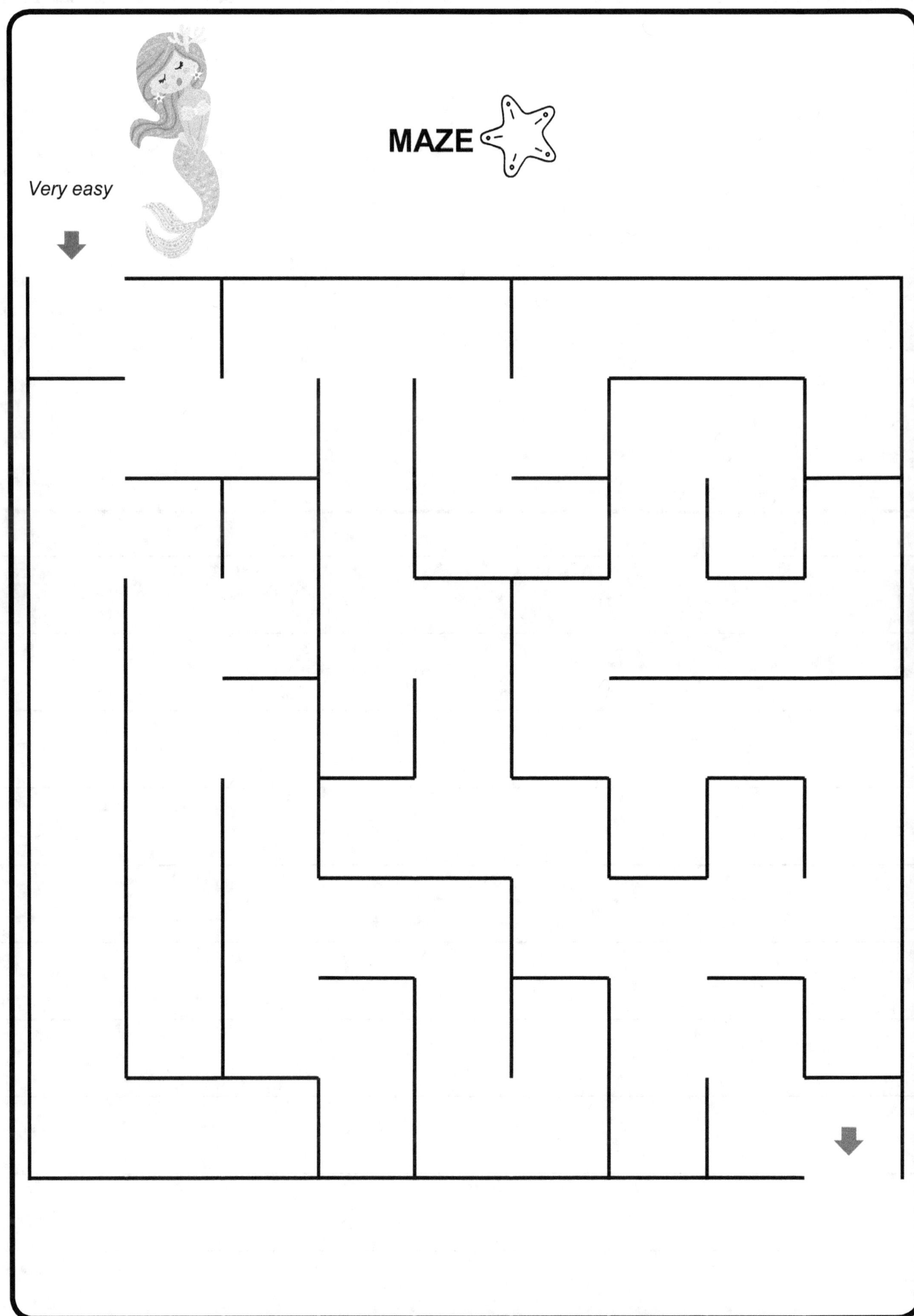
Very easy
MAZE

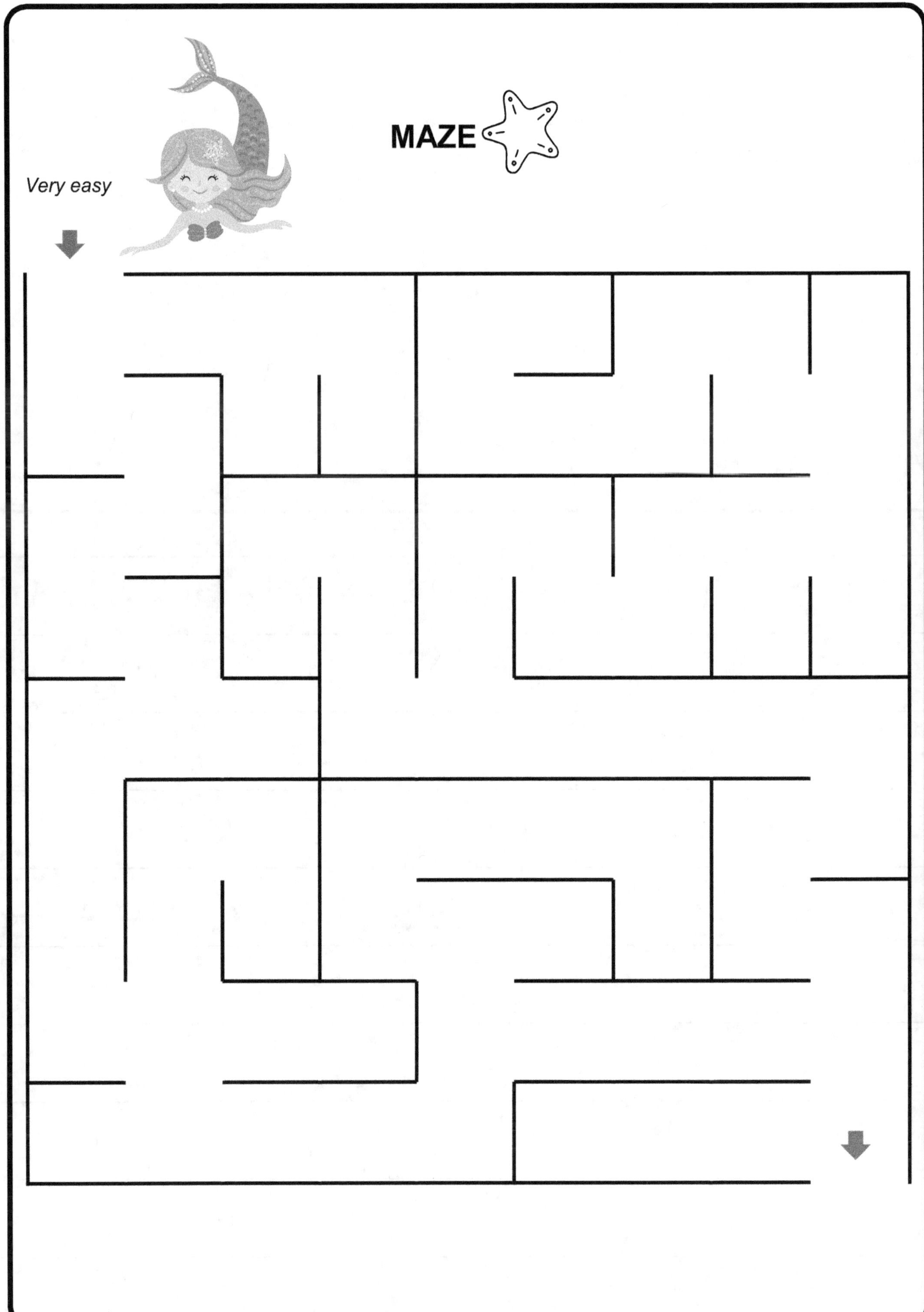
MAZE
Very easy

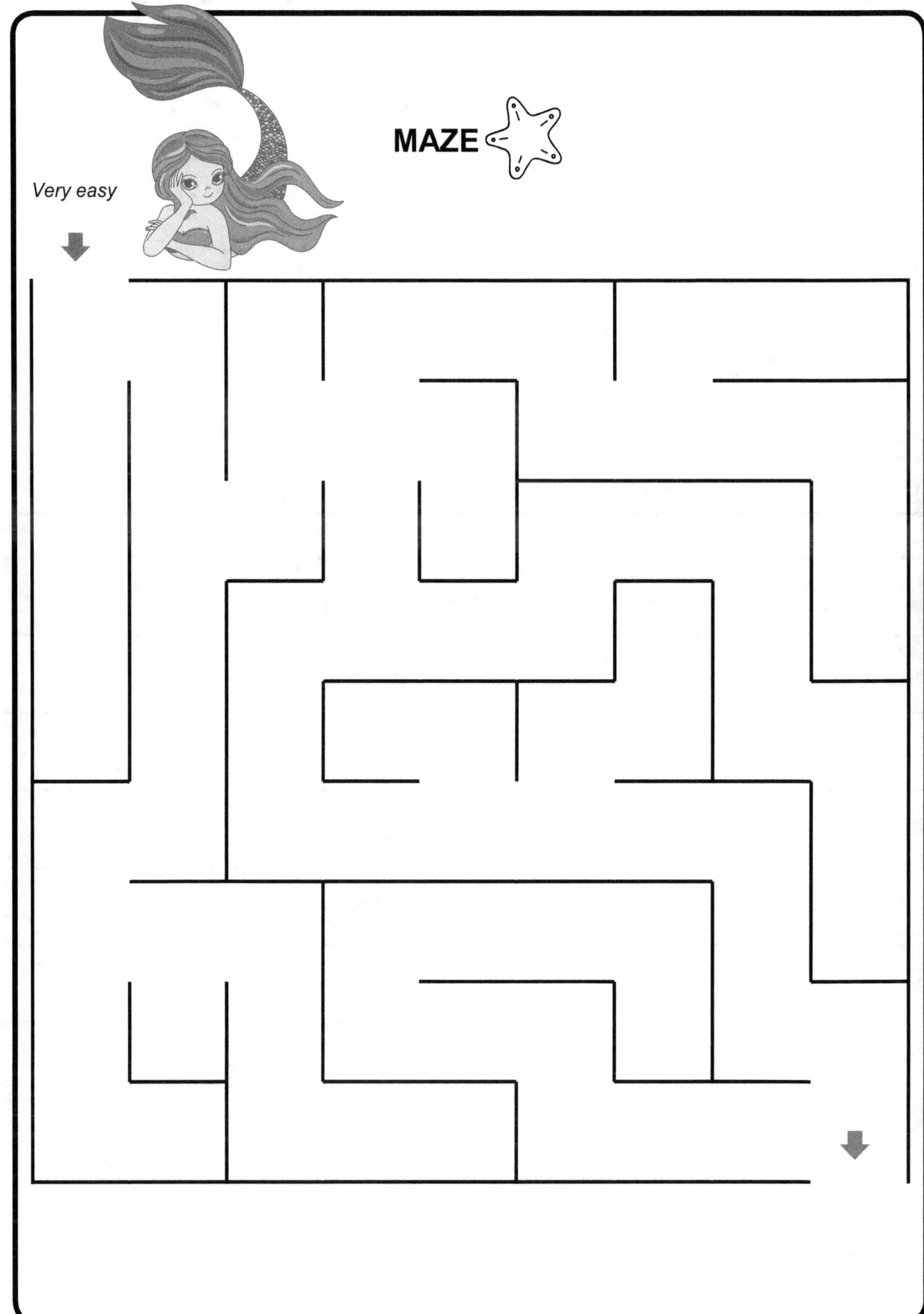
MAZE
Very easy

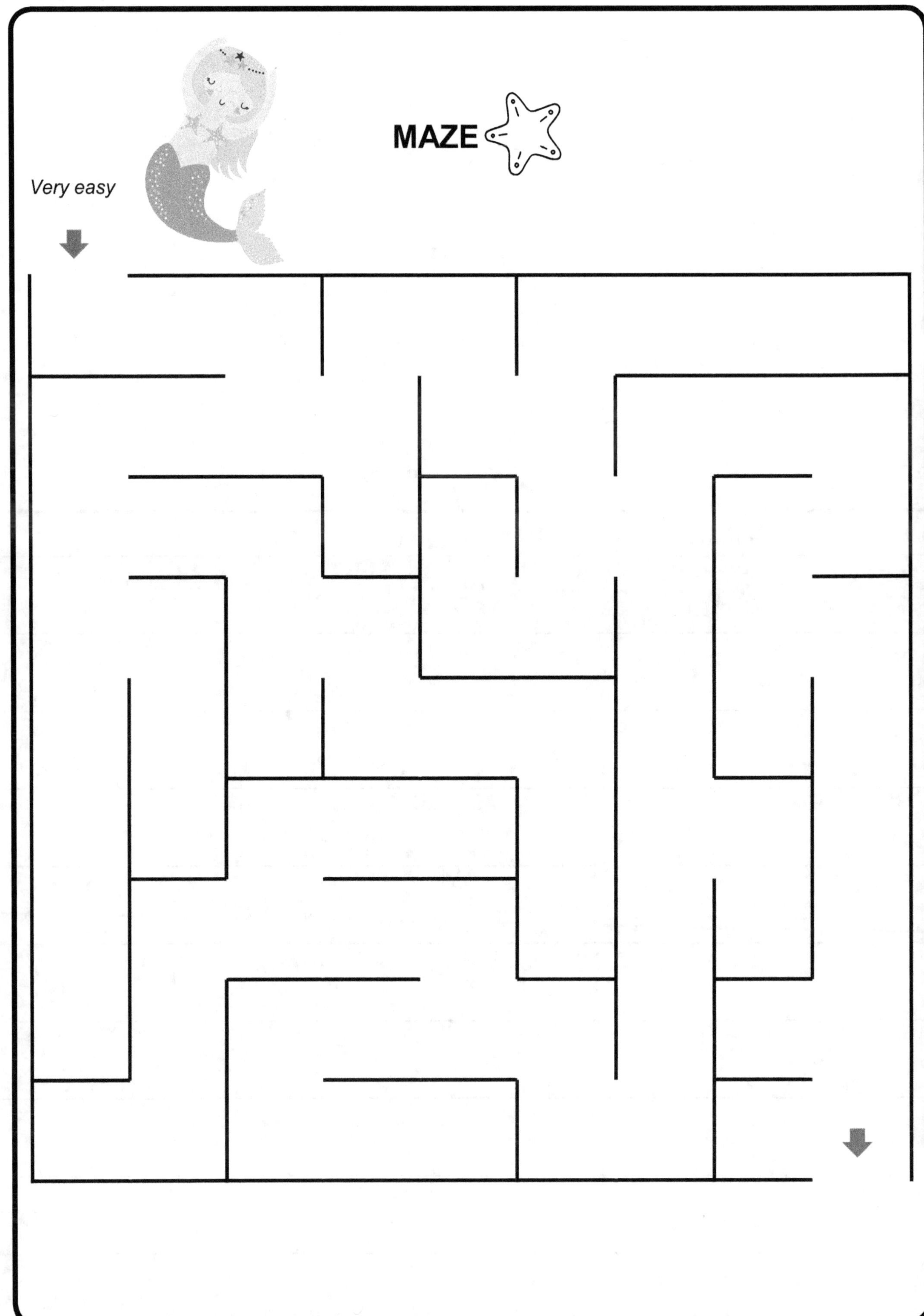
MAZE
Very easy

Very easy
MAZE

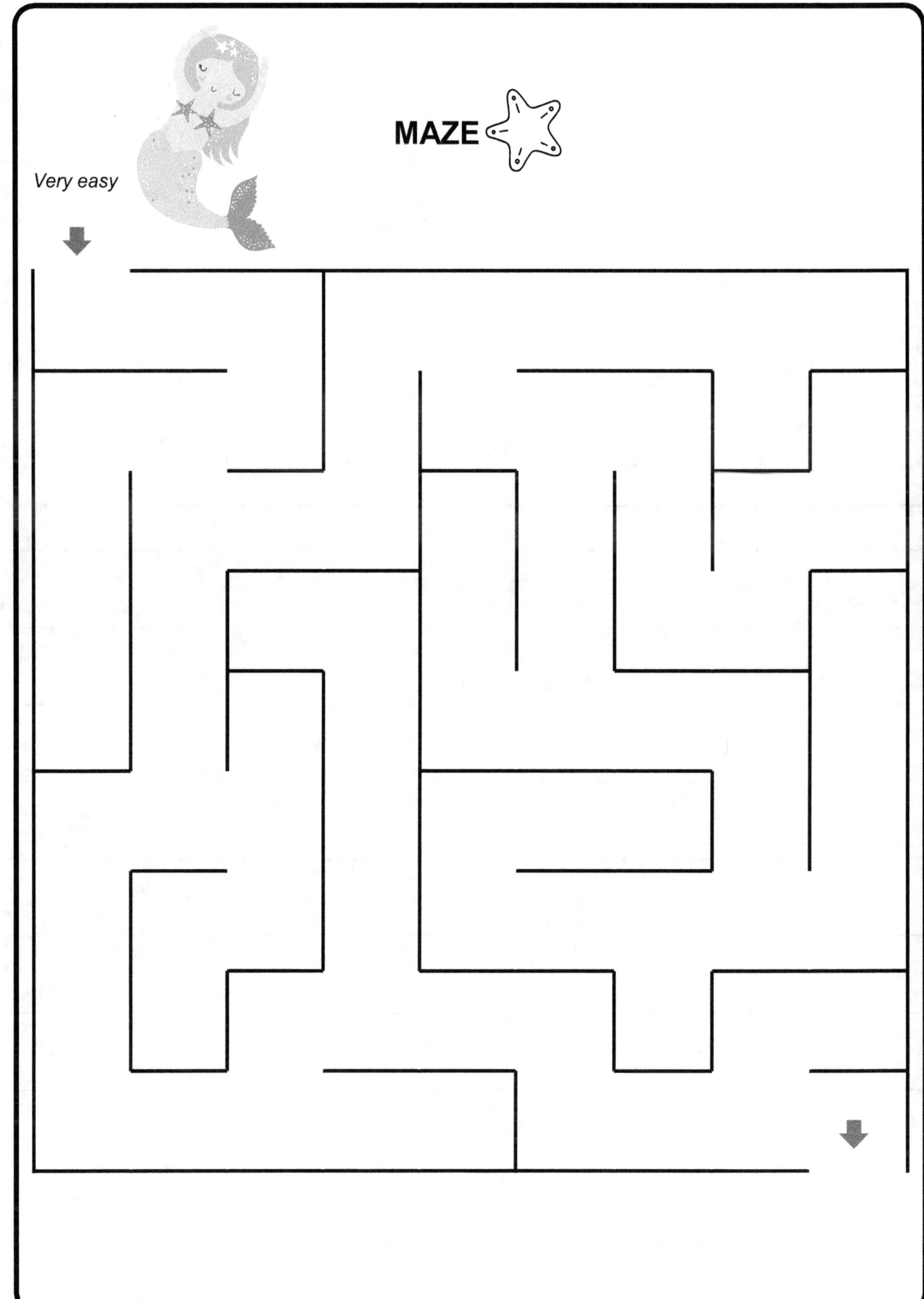
MAZE
Very easy

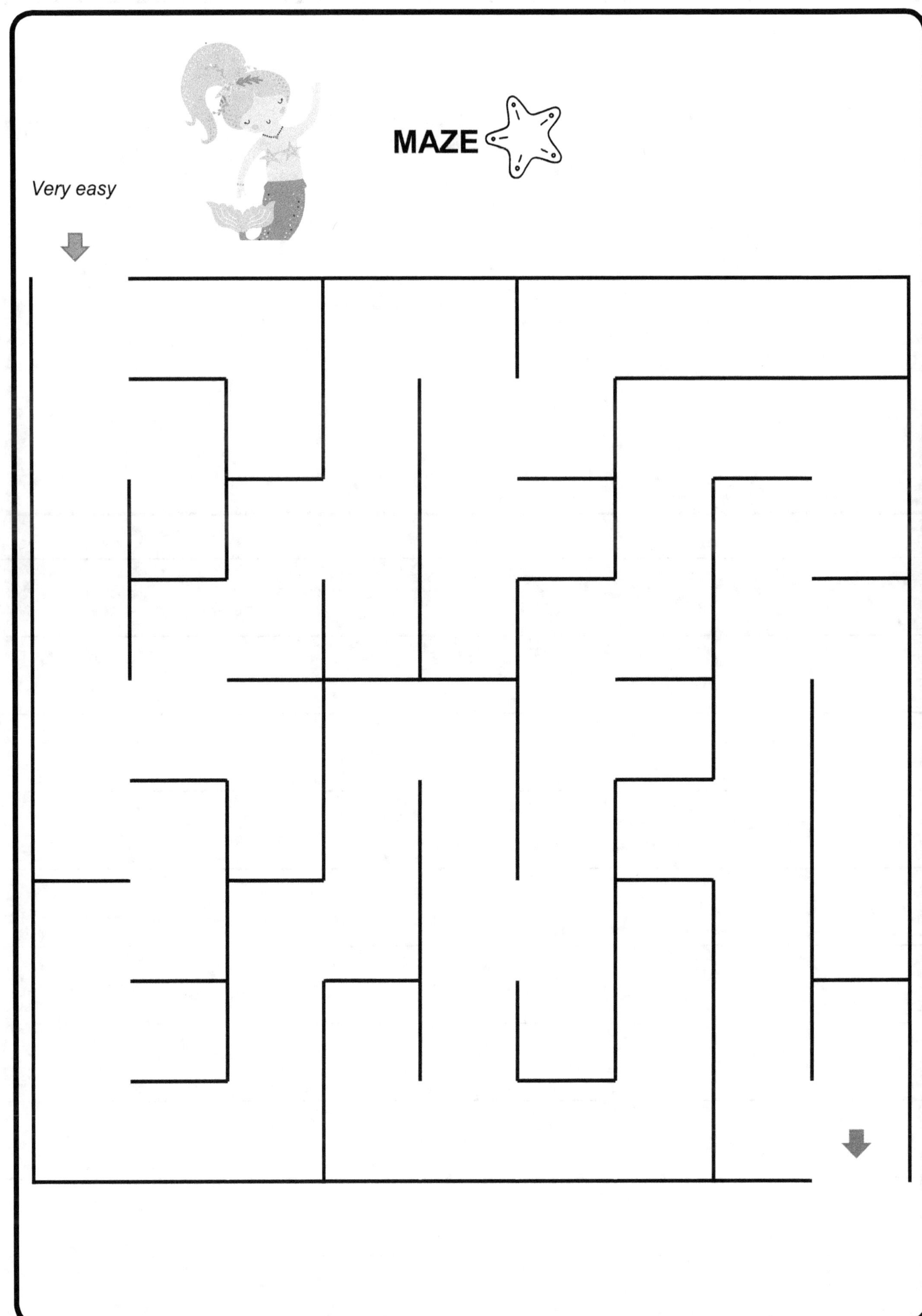
MAZE
Very easy

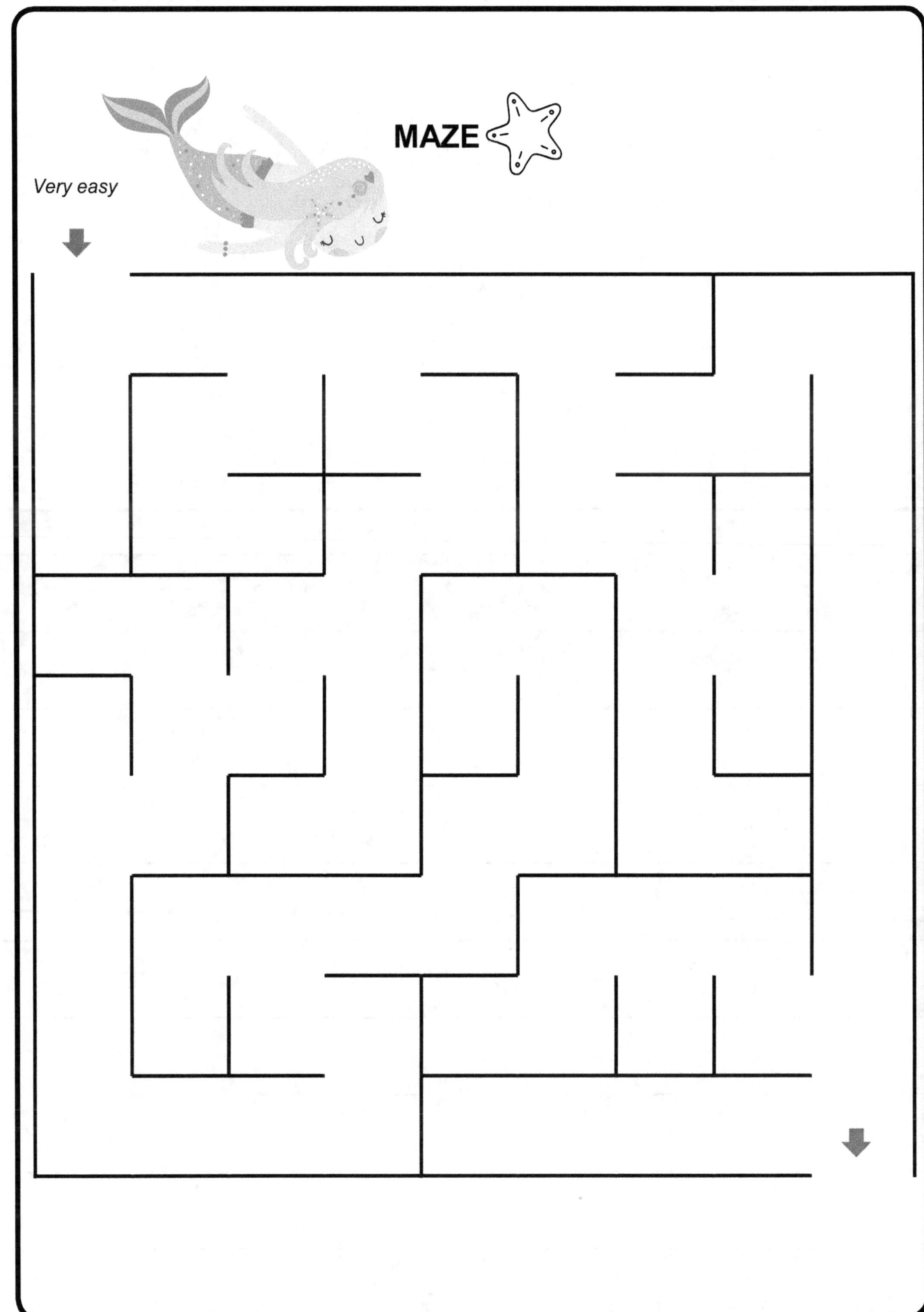
MAZE
Very easy

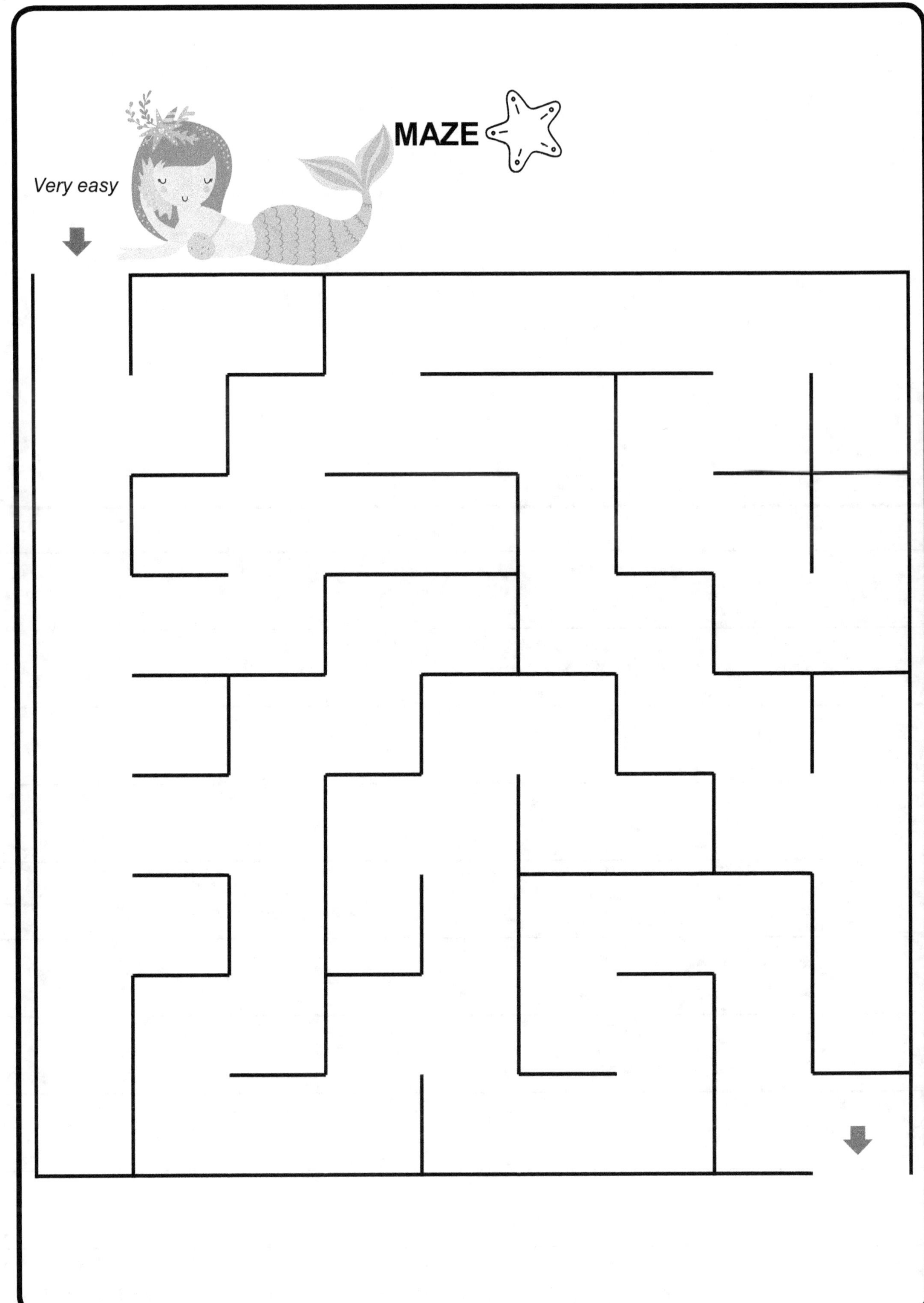
MAZE
Very easy

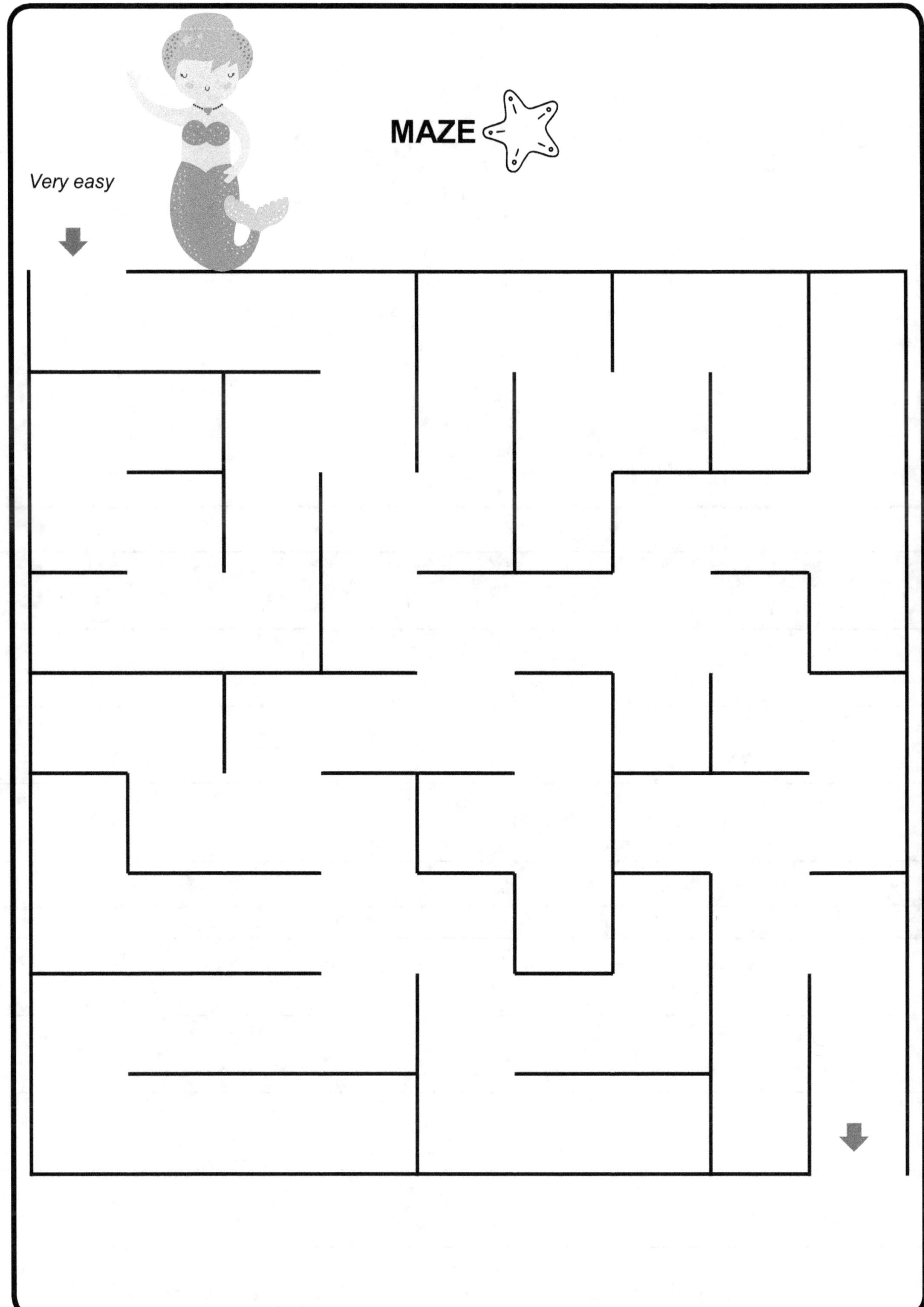
MAZE
Very easy

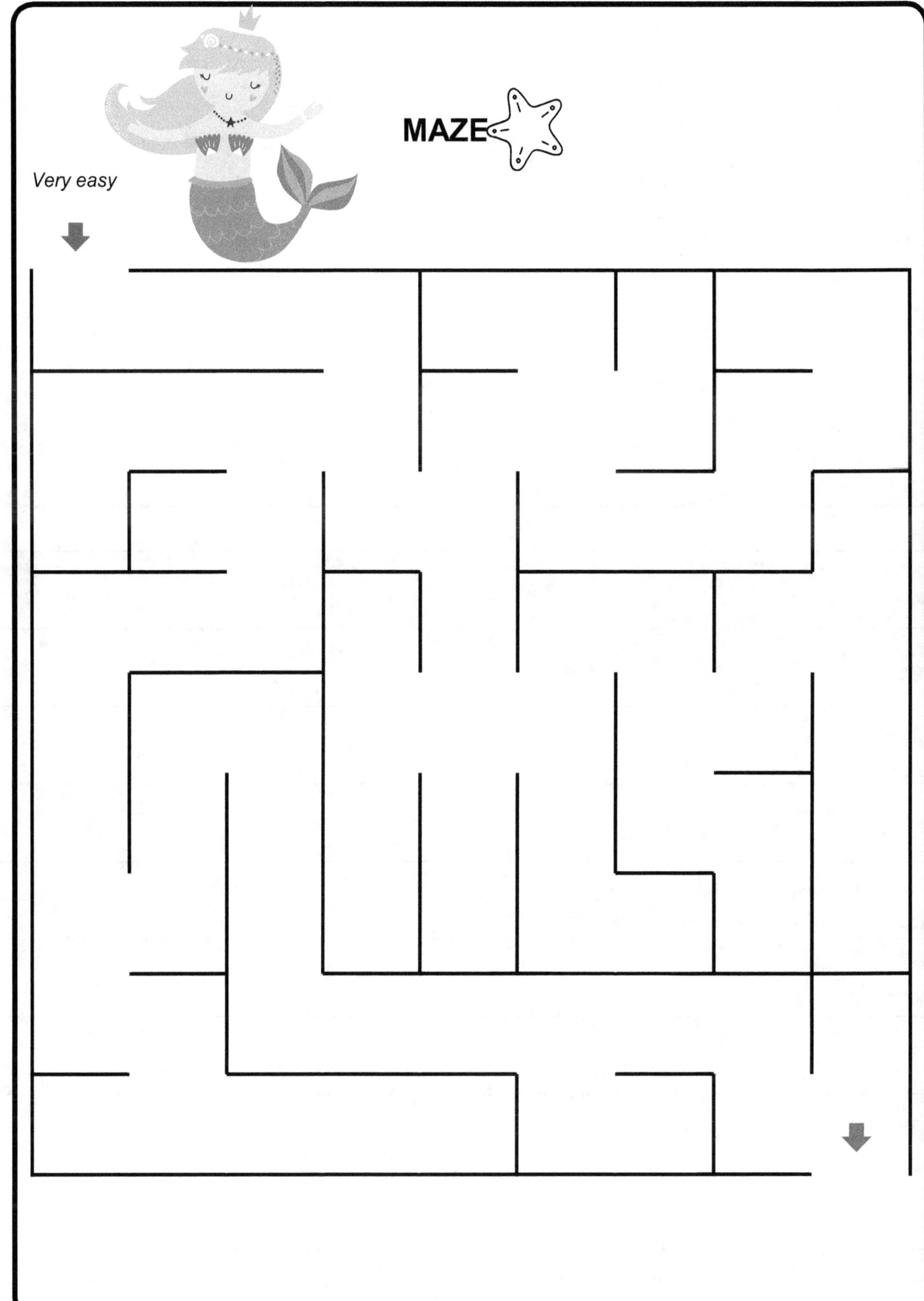

MAZE
Very easy

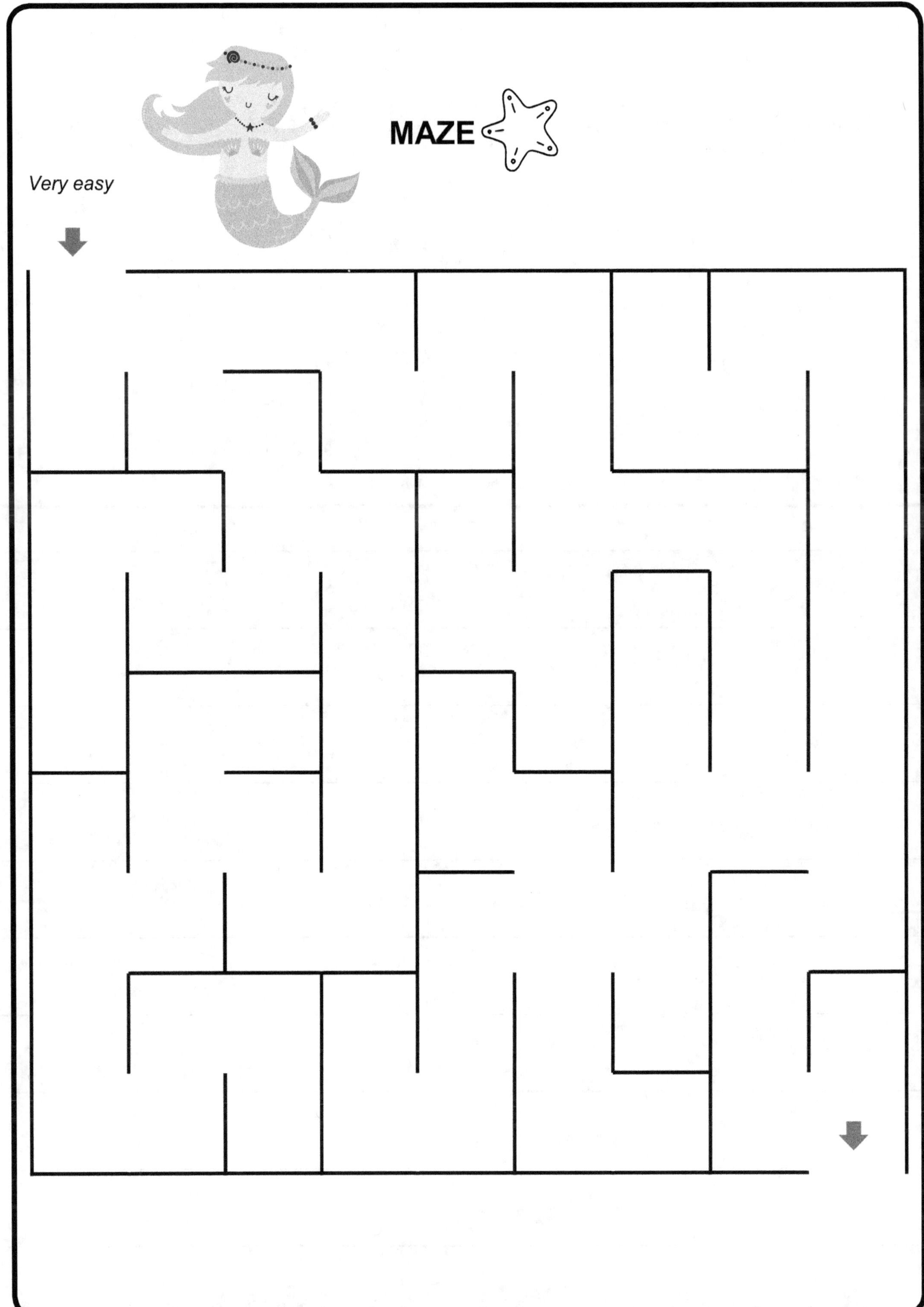
MAZE
Very easy

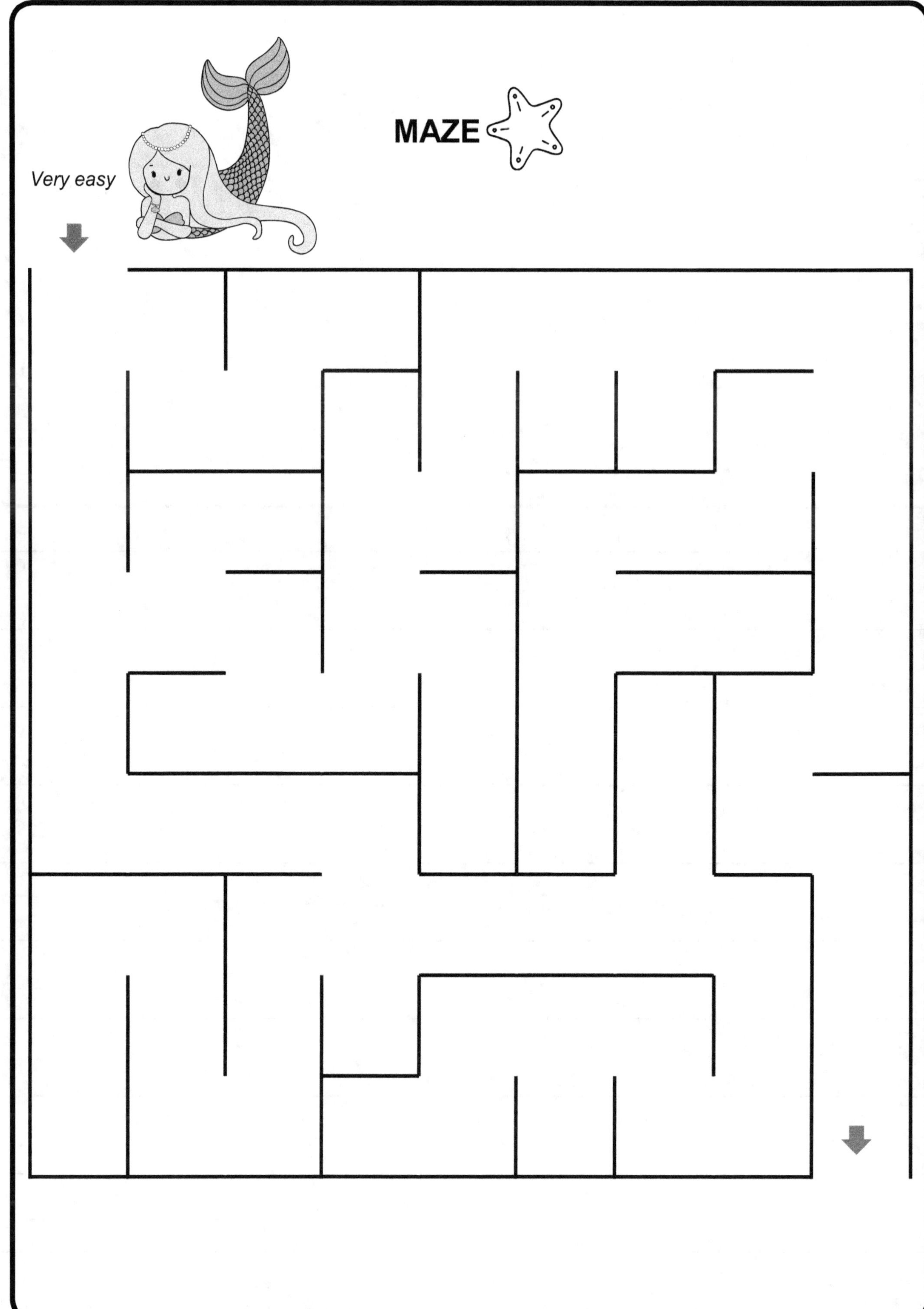
MAZE
Very easy

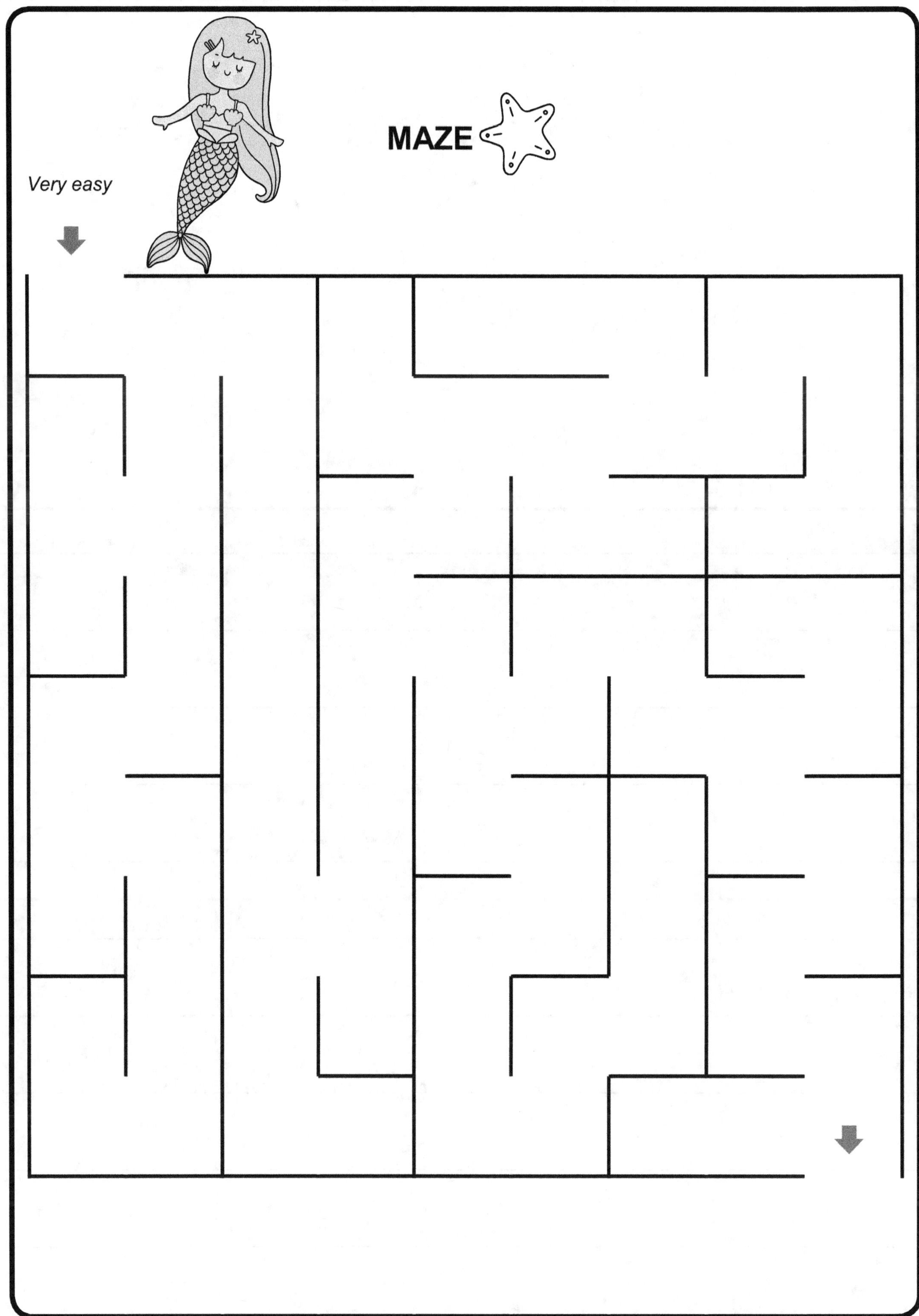
MAZE
Very easy

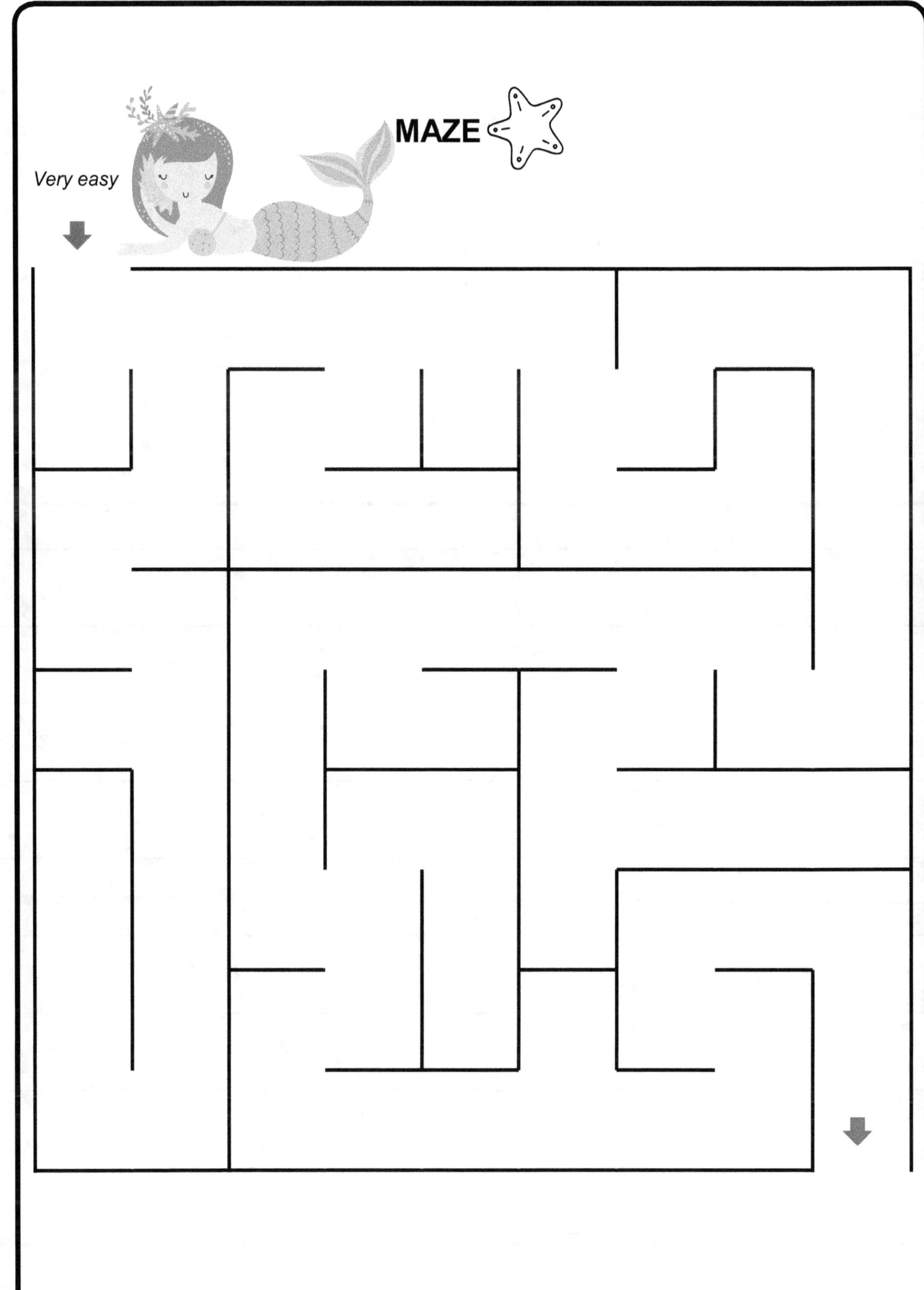
Very easy
MAZE

MAZE
Very easy

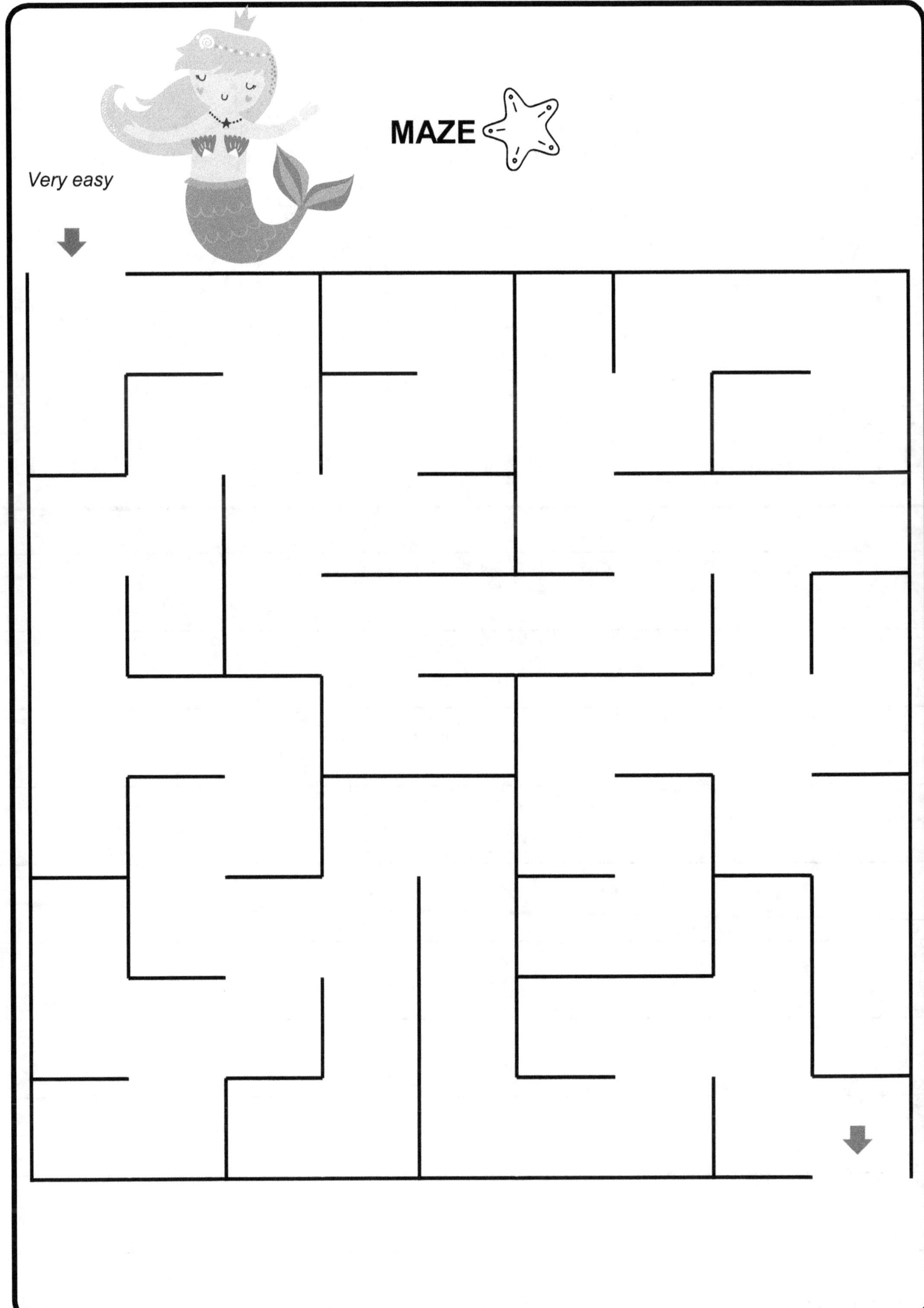

MAZE
Very easy

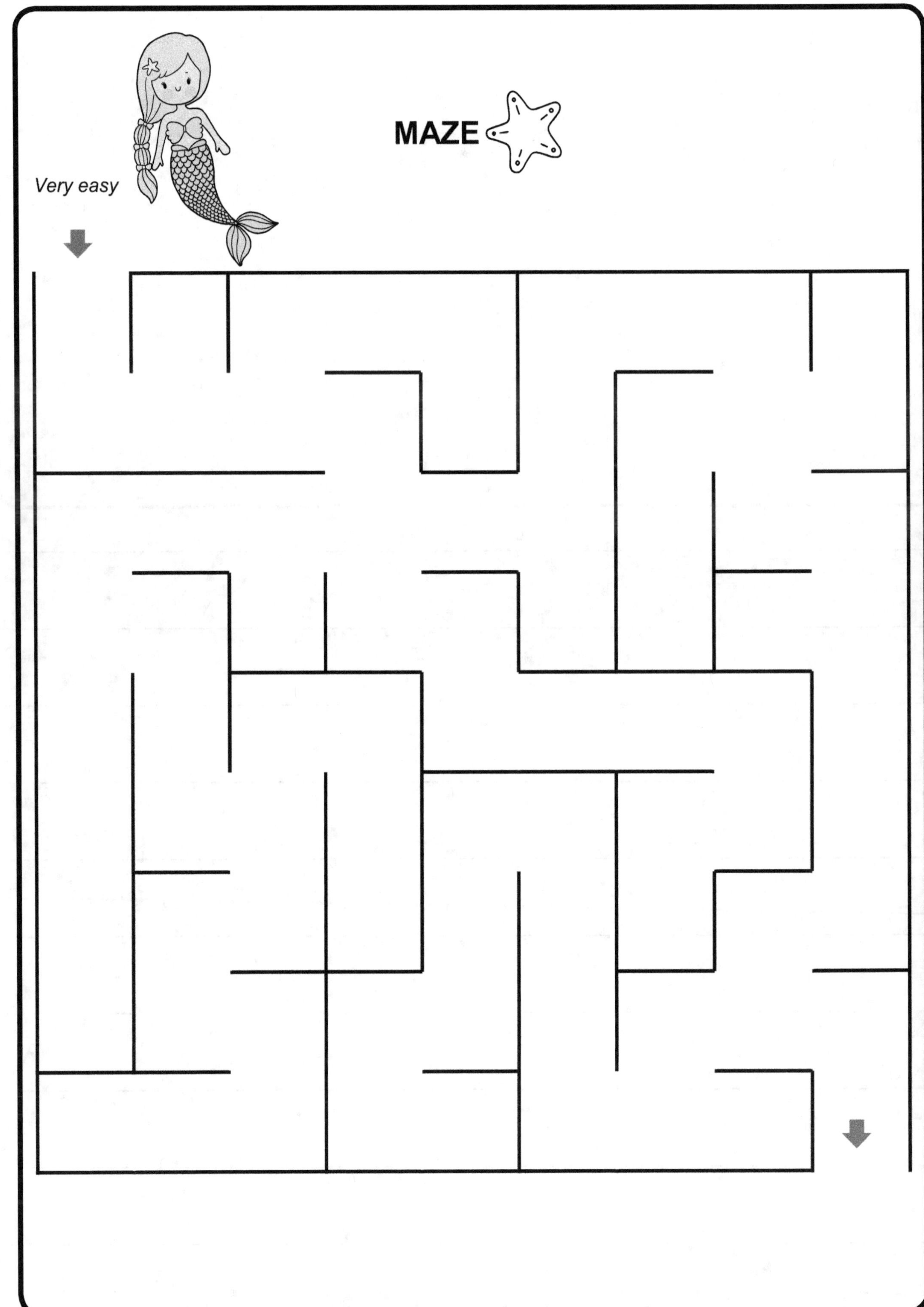
MAZE
Very easy

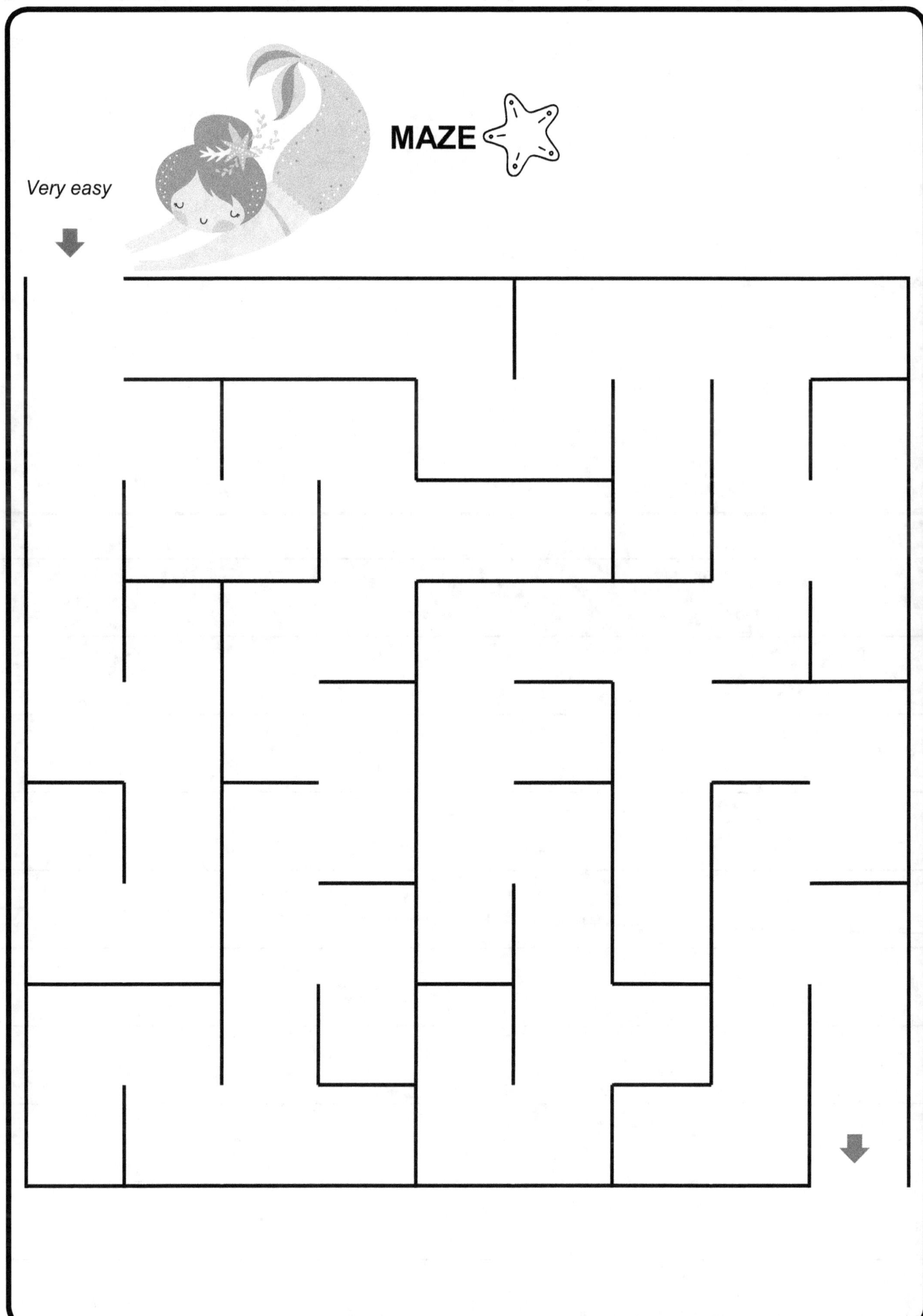

MAZE
Very easy

www.ingramcontent.com/pod-product-compliance
Lightning Source LLC
LaVergne TN
LVHW080816170826
845678LV00011B/2033

* 9 7 9 8 4 5 8 0 1 5 6 1 5 *